THEY CAME FROM CENTER FIELD

by
DAN GUTMAN

Illustrated by
JEFF LINDBERG

A
LITTLE APPLE
PAPERBACK

SCHOLASTIC INC.
New York Toronto London Auckland Sydney

In memory of Sid Gutman

ISBN 0-590-47975-X

12 11 10 9 8 7 6 5 4 3 2 1   5 6 7 8 9/9 0/0

Printed in the U.S.A.   40

First Scholastic printing, March 1995

Contents

1
A Flash in the Sky

It was one of those summer evenings, the kind where it's so hot that your hand sticks inside your baseball glove from the sweat. The gang and I were playing a friendly baseball game against some kids from Tatum School on the field over at Crow's Woods, a mile outside of town.

No uniforms, no parents getting in the way and yelling and screaming advice or anything. It was just for the fun of it. We had ridden our bikes over there after dinner. It was getting too dark to see the ball, but nobody wanted to be the first to say we should go home.

My true love is sports. I could wake up in the morning, play ball all day long until it gets dark, and then go to sleep and do it all over again. Every day. Boy, that would be great. Of course, I can't do that because I have to eat and go to school and do other stuff that cuts into my ball playing time. But I can dream, can't I?

On this night, I was pitching. I don't want to brag or anything, but I'm better at sports than most. Other kids look up to me, I guess, and my teachers always say, "That Bloop Jones is a natural leader." I don't really try to do anything special. I just act naturally.

Our team usually wins. Well, to be honest, we *always* win. We call ourselves "The SBDs." Silent But Deadly.

But I wasn't much of a leader this night. I had given up eight runs. Fortunately, we had scored nine. It was the ninth inning, the bases were loaded with two out. It wasn't looking good for the SBDs.

I checked the runner at first. He wasn't going anywhere. I glanced at the runner on second, and looked the runner back to third, and leaned in for the sign.

My catcher, Charles "Corny" Kornbluth, put down one finger. On every square inch of the planet Earth, a finger pointing down means one thing.

Fastball.

Or at least it looked as if Corny was asking for a fastball. It was getting so dark, I could barely see my own hand in front of my face.

"Hey, Corny!" I yelled out. "How many fingers are you puttin' down?"

"Two!" Corny shouted back. "You know what that means?"

"I think so." Two fingers means curveball.

This was all planned to fool the batter, mind you. Corny and I had a little arrangement. Any time I would call out for the sign, Corny would say the opposite sign. So if Corny said, "Two," that meant one, and if he said, "One," that meant two.

We saved this trick for tough situations — like this one. Bases loaded, two outs, one run lead, ninth inning.

Mitch Wallace, the best hitter for Tatum, dug in at the plate. I already had two strikes on him.

"Bases loaded, two outs, one run lead, ninth inning," I said to myself. "Bases loaded, two outs, one run lead, ninth inning."

Mitch wiped his hands on his pants and twisted the bat. He looked at me as if he could taste the RBIs he was about to get.

"Mitch, you can't touch this," I said as I gripped the ball across the seams.

4

"You'd better duck after you throw it," Mitch fired back. "I don't want you to get hurt when a line drive goes directly at the spot your head once occupied."

"Tell you what," I shouted as I went into my windup. "Whichever one of us is wrong has to push a peanut around the bases — with his nose."

"You're on, hot dog."

Saying stupid insults at each other is part of the fun of baseball, I think. I kicked my right leg up high, the way I'd seen Juan Marichal do it. I rocked back on my left leg and came over the top, whipping the ball at the plate with every ounce of energy I could muster.

Mitch, expecting a slow curve, stood there with his mouth open as the ball popped into Corny's mitt.

"Strike three!" Corny crowed.

"No *way* that was a strike!" Mitch argued.

"The catcher calls balls and strikes, Mitch," I yelled.

"I'll get you, Bloop Jones!" shouted Mitch angrily. He slammed the bat against the plate.

"I'll get you, too, Mitch," I laughed. "I'll get you a peanut." I reached into my pocket, pulled one out, and flipped it to him. Everybody broke up laughing.

But just then, something totally amazing happened that shut us all up. Out beyond the center field fence there was a sudden blinding flash of light. A second or two later, three loud *boooooooms* echoed in the night.

The sky was clear. It wasn't a thunderstorm. There was something else going on out there.

"Hit the dirt!" Mitch screamed. Mitch, of course, had *already* hit the dirt.

"Air raid!" somebody shouted.

"Maybe a plane crashed!" yelled Sally Garber, our second baseman.

"I'm scared!" moaned Ray Robles, our right fielder, who gets scared by just about anything.

"Maybe it's a flying saucer," Corny added. He began whistling the theme music from *The Twilight Zone* and making funny vibration noises with his mouth. Did you ever hear a joke that was so unfunny it was funny? Corny's always cracking jokes like that, and that's how he got the nickname "Corny."

"Knock it off, Corny," Sally said sternly.

"Let's check it out," I said.

"You check it out. I'm outta here," muttered Mitch. He got up off the ground, tossed the peanut back to me, and walked off the field. What would the other Tatum kids do? They were all looking at each other, shrugging their shoulders. First one, and then the whole bunch of them, ran off the field following Mitch.

"Chickens!" shouted Ray after them. "You Tatum guys are yellow!" Ray loved it when somebody else was afraid of something for a change.

"Buck buck buck buck buck buck!" added Corny in his best chicken imitation. Corny could imitate just about anything, from farm animals to the President of the United States.

"Fine," I said as the Tatum guys disappeared down the road on their bikes. "Let 'em go. But I want to see what's out there. Are any of you scared, too? Maybe you'd better leave now — while you can still get out . . . alive."

I looked at Ray. He wasn't moving. Sally, Corny, and the rest of the SBDs stood their ground. "Good," I said proudly. "I'll bet we find something really cool that we can bring to science class tomorrow!"

There was no turning back.

Man, what was I getting us into? On the inside, I was just as scared as everybody else. Who knows what might be out there? It was getting late and I should have been home an hour earlier. My mom was going to throw a fit for sure. But who can resist an adventure?

"Onward, team!" I shouted. "The light was beyond center field!"

Our adventure was about to begin. One by one, each of us dug a sneaker into the outfield fence and leaped over, running into the thickening darkness of Crow's Woods.

2
Contact

The path through Crow's Woods was winding, so it wasn't long before we lost sight of the baseball field. The full moon made it a little easier to find our way around, but we had no idea where the noise and flash of light had come from.

Except for the sound of the leaves crunching under our feet, it was dead quiet now. Ray was turning around to look behind him with every step, and Sally had this worried expression on her face. For once, Corny wasn't cracking his usual jokes. I was sure the whole gang would have headed for home along with Mitch's team if I hadn't pretended to be so brave.

The path wound around a corner and I could see a clearing up ahead. With hand motions, I signaled for everybody to stay low, keep quiet, and to follow me. It's amazing how much you can communicate without saying a word. We couldn't have gone more than ten feet when we saw it.

"Look!" Sally whispered, pointing. Everybody gasped.

Three triangular-shaped spaceships, each the size of a small house, hovered a foot or so off the ground. They seemed to be metallic, but were colored dark blue like the night sky. Bright lights blinked on and off in irregular patterns. A steady humming sound came out of the ships, which seemed to be rotating. It wasn't a windy night, but the trees around the clearing rustled. The grass beneath the ships was flattened and charred.

My mouth dropped open. Was it real? I felt shivering goose bumps up and down my arms. This kind of thing was supposed to happen in science fiction movies, I thought to myself, not in the real world.

"Nobody's gonna believe this!" I whispered to Sally. "How do we know we're not dreaming?"

"Everybody's going to say we're crazy," Sally replied. "But I see it. You see it. We all see what we're seeing."

We stopped whispering when a ramp suddenly dropped from each ship and came to rest on the ground. The humming noise grew quieter, the lights dimmed slightly. After a few seconds, it appeared as though some activity was going on at the top of each ramp.

Suddenly, three box-shaped objects — about the size of soda machines — slid slowly down the ramp of each ship and came to a stop at the bottom, where they hovered a few inches off the ground.

"They must be unloading their cargo," Sally whispered in my ear.

After nine boxes had reached the ground, the ramps rose up again, sealing the space-ships.

"Why don't they come out?" Sally wondered aloud. "What are they afraid of?"

"Maybe they're afraid of us," I whispered. "Maybe we should come out and show them we're friendly."

"You go out there and show 'em, Bloop," said Ray nervously. "I can be perfectly friendly from behind this bush."

"Okay, I will."

"Bloop, you are *soooo* brave, man," Corny said. "Brave and dumb."

"If anything happens to me, Corny," I said, handing him my mitt, "I want you to have this to remember me by."

"Thanks, Bloop," Corny said, "but I'd rather have your baseball card collection."

I stood up slowly and stepped over a bush into the clearing, putting my hands up over my head so it was obvious that I wasn't carrying any weapon — just like in the movies.

I couldn't stop my hands from shaking. My nose was itching, but I didn't dare drop a hand down to scratch it. I walked slowly toward the triangular spaceships.

"We . . . are . . . friendly," I called out. "Please . . . do . . . not . . . harm . . . us." I repeated this a few times as I walked around the big boxes. Looking more closely at them, I could see that each one had a row of flashing lights around the top and a hole in its middle about the size of a big jar of peanut butter.

The boxes hovered a few inches above the ground, but there didn't seem to be any fans

or jets of air that were keeping them up. Everything was quiet, except for a steady *woooooshing* noise.

"Please come out!" I shouted more confidently. "We are friendly. Why don't you come out?"

"WE *ARE* OUT!" said a voice from one of the boxes.

I jumped about three feet in the air, landing on my backside in the dirt next to one of the boxes. The boxes, I finally realized, *were* the aliens. My careful reading of thousands of comic books over the years hadn't prepared me for anything quite like this. I'd always thought aliens would be little green men with skinny arms and legs and large heads with funny-looking eyes — not levitating Coke machines.

"ARE YOU THE LEADER OF THIS PLANET?" asked one of the boxes.

"N-n-no. I am just a boy," I replied. "My

16

name is Bloop Jones. So you speak English on your planet?"

"NO. WE MONITORED YOUR RADIO AND TV FREQUENCIES ON OUR JOURNEY HERE AND ASSIMILATED YOUR LANGUAGE."

Assimilated? I've been listening to English for twelve *years* and I didn't know what *that* meant. This guy learned the whole dictionary on the ride over.

"ASSIMILATE," the box stated dryly. "TO ABSORB AS NOURISHMENT. TO UNDERSTAND."

By now, the rest of the gang had come out from behind the bushes and gathered around the nine big boxes in a large circle. Nine of us and nine of them, I noticed. We could play a game of baseball. Unless, of course, they would rather just kill us.

"These are my friends," I said, pointing to each one. "Corny, Sally, Ray, Billy, Lucy, Roger, Mike, and Brian." The boxes didn't respond, so I asked, "Do you have names?"

"IT WOULD BE IMPOSSIBLE FOR EARTHLINGS

TO REPRODUCE OUR NAMES WITH YOUR PRIM-
ITIVE VOCAL ABILITIES," he said. "THEREFORE,
WE HAVE MONITORED YOUR TRANSMISSIONS
AND CHOSEN NAMES YOU CAN UNDERSTAND.
MY NAME IS MCDONALD."

"How about we call you Mack?" suggested Sally.

"IF YOU WISH," Mack said.

"What about your comrades?" I asked.
"What do you call them?"

"I AM CALLED WENDY," said one. She must
be a female, I figured, even though there
was no way to tell one alien from another.

"I AM CALLED BURGER KING," said another.

"I AM CALLED TACO BELL," said a third.

"Are you related to Albert Belle?" asked
Corny jokingly. The alien didn't answer.

"I AM CALLED PIZZA HUT," droned a fourth.

"I'm starved," Corny chimed after each
one had rattled off the name of a different

fast-food chain. "You guys don't by any chance dispense munchies out of those holes, do you?"

"MUNCHIES?" asked Mack. "WE HAVE NOT ENCOUNTERED THIS TERM."

"Forget it," Sally said. "Where are you from?"

"WE ARE FROM A PLANET YOU HAVE NEVER HEARD OF," Mack said. "WE HAVE TRAVELED TWENTY-FIVE LIGHT-YEARS TO VISIT YOU."

"What's that in dog years?" asked Corny.

"ONE LIGHT-YEAR IS APPROXIMATELY SIX MILLION MILLION MILES."

"Oh yeah?" Corny replied. "Well, a dog year is seven human years."

"Wow!" Sally said, taking out her pocket calculator. "Your planet is . . . let me see . . . a hundred and fifty million million miles from Earth!"

"Let me ask you a question," Corny said. "How come you guys always show up in the middle of nowhere? Why don't you land on the White House lawn or in New York City or something? You'd be in all the papers and on the evening news."

"ENOUGH," Mack replied. "WE HAVE A MISSION TO COMPLETE."

"What sort of mission?" I asked. "What have you come for? Do you want our gold?"

"NO, THAT IS A WORTHLESS SUBSTANCE."

"Try telling my parents that," Corny cracked.

"Have you come for our weapons?" I suggested.

"NO. YOUR PRIMITIVE WEAPONS ARE PEA SHOOTERS COMPARED WITH THE TECHNOLOGY WE HAVE ON OUR PLANET."

"Then what is it?" Sally demanded.

"BASEBALL," Mack answered.

"Baseball?!" we all asked incredulously.

"BASEBALL," Mack said seriously. "WE WANT BASEBALL."

"Don't you have sporting goods stores on your planet?" asked Ray. This was the first thing he'd said to the aliens. Ray's dad owned a sporting goods store.

"Here, you can have a ball," Sally said, flipping one toward Mack. "No charge." A gust of air shot out of the hole in Mack's belly, and he sucked the ball into the hole like a vacuum cleaner. I noticed that he caught it on the fly.

"You came twenty-five light-years for a baseball?" Ray asked.

"What he means is, he wants to take the game of baseball back to his people," I reasoned. "Am I right?"

"CORRECT. FROM CAREFULLY RESEARCHING YOUR CIVILIZATION, WE HAVE DETERMINED THAT THE ONLY THING WORTH SAVING IS BASEBALL."

"What about Beethoven's Ninth Symphony?" asked Sally. "What about paintings from the Renaissance? Einstein's

Theory of Relativity? Twinkies?"

"RUBBISH," Mack said firmly. "WE JUST WANT BASEBALL."

"If you're so smart," I said, "why didn't you assimilate baseball on your way over? After all, you learned the whole English language."

"WE TRIED," replied Mack. "BALLS, STRIKES, FOUL TIPS, BALKS, HIT-AND-RUN. TOO COMPLICATED. OUR COMPUTERS COULD NOT PROCESS SO MUCH INFORMATION."

"We'll teach you how to play baseball," Corny said. "No problem."

"Wait a minute!" I slapped a hand over Corny's mouth. "We've got to have a little powwow here."

I pulled the gang aside and gathered them around me in a huddle.

"Bloop, what's the big deal?" whispered Sally. "Let's show them how to play. It'll be a blast. I can't wait to tell everybody at school."

"Do you really think anybody at school is going to believe this?" I said. "Listen, you guys. Let's think about this for a second. We've got something they want. Something they want badly enough to travel twenty-five light-years. So in all fairness, they should give us something we want, right?"

After a few minutes the huddle broke up and we approached Mack and his crew, who were hovering around the bats and gloves curiously.

"OK, we'll make a deal with you," I said.

"WHAT KIND OF DEAL?" Mack asked.

"We'll teach you everything we know about baseball — if you let us have one of your flying saucers."

"ABSOLUTELY NOT!" shouted the one who called himself Taco Bell. "THEY ARE THE PROPERTY OF OUR PLANET'S SPACE PROGRAM."

"WAIT A MINUTE!" Mack said. "WE MUST DISCUSS THIS PROPOSAL."

The aliens hovered back about ten feet and gathered together in a huddle of their own. We stood there watching and listening to the mixture of lights and beeps that made up the aliens' language, but it didn't make any sense to us.

I knew they would never give us one of their spaceships, but they might give us *something*. That's how negotiations work, right? After about a minute of flashing and beeping, the aliens slid forward and approached us.

"WE HAVE A COUNTERPROPOSAL," Mack said. "YOU TEACH US HOW TO PLAY BASEBALL. THEN WE WILL PLAY A GAME. IF YOU WIN THE GAME, YOU CAN HAVE A RIDE ON ONE OF OUR SHIPS."

"Deal!" I quickly replied. How could we lose to these Coke machines?

As Sally and Ray went to get the balls and bats, I walked over to where Mack was hovering and whispered, "What if we had refused to show you how to play baseball?"

Mack's lights flashed as he spoke. "THEN WE WOULD HAVE BEEN FORCED TO DESTROY YOUR PLANET."

3
The Fine Points of the Game

It was dark now, except for the full moon hanging in the sky. We knew our parents were home worrying, but who could resist an adventure like this one? I mean, how many times in your life do you get the chance to play ball with creatures from outer space?

Mack and his crew slid back up the ramps into their spaceships. We watched as the ships rose off the ground one at a time and flew over the trees of Crow's Woods to the baseball field.

They flew straight up like helicopters do, but in complete silence. They must have been powered by some force like magnetism that doesn't require an engine that burns something to generate power.

We were all excited as we made our way through the woods. Even Ray had forgotten how afraid he was. Now all we wanted to do was play ball.

The three spaceships took up positions in left field, center field, and right field, just beyond the fence. Their bright lights lit up the diamond with an eerie glow, like giant flashlights covered with colored cellophane. The aliens slid out of the ships once again and everyone gathered around me at home plate.

"Now listen up, everybody," I said. "Baseball is a very simple game. Any six-year-old Earth kid knows how to play it, so with your superior intelligence you should be able to pick it up in a few minutes.

"First things first. The object of the game is to score runs — more runs than your opponent."

"HOW DOES ONE SCORE A RUN?" one of the aliens asked.

"When you step on this thing called home plate, you score a run."

Hearing that, the alien who called himself Burger King slid over to home plate and dropped down on top of it.

"THERE," he said proudly. "I HAVE SCORED ONE RUN. WE ARE WINNING! I *LOVE* THIS PLACE!"

"No, no!" I explained. "You have to step on first, second, and third base first." I pointed out the locations of the other bases.

Burger King took off like a shot, hovering his way to first, second, third, and home. He moved pretty fast for a soda machine.

"THAT'S ANOTHER RUN! WE ARE NOW WINNING TWO TO ZERO."

I glanced at Corny, and he rolled his eyes. "If this is what they call 'superior intelligence,'" Corny whispered, "I'd rather be a dumb Earthling."

I picked up a bat and ball and held them up in the air. "Umm, perhaps baseball isn't quite as simple as I led you to believe," I said. "Let me back up a little. You see, this round thing is a ball. And this long stick is a bat. Is everybody following?"

"YOUR GAME OF GOLF USES A BALL AND A STICK," said Mack. "SO DOES TENNIS, CRICKET, LACROSSE, AND HOCKEY."

"Actually, they use a puck in hockey," I replied. "Now listen up. The pitcher stands on that mound over there and throws the ball toward the plate. The hitter — the one holding the bat — tries to hit the ball hard enough so the team in the field can't reach it. If he hits the ball and reaches first base, that's a single. If he reaches second base, that's a double. If he reaches third base, it's

a triple. And if he makes it all the way around, that's a — "

"QUADRUPLE!" said Mack triumphantly.

"Well, we call it a home run," I continued. "But that was a good guess. Now, while the team at bat is trying to hit the ball and run around the bases, the team in the field is trying to stop them. Get it? If they can catch a batted ball before it hits the ground, that's an out. If the ball is hit on the ground, they can make an out if they field it and throw it to first base before the hitter gets there. After they make three outs, the two teams switch places."

"WHY IS IT THAT A BALL HIT ON THE GROUND MUST BE THROWN TO FIRST BASE WHILE A BALL CAUGHT IN THE AIR MUST NOT?"

I thought about the question, and in a few moments my lightning brain had discerned the answer. "Because those are the rules," I said.

"ON OUR PLANET, EVENTS OCCUR IN AN ORGANIZED, LOGICAL SEQUENCE," Mack said. "ON OUR PLANET, THINGS MUST MAKE SENSE BEFORE THEY BECOME RULES."

"Boy, are you ever in the wrong galaxy," Corny said.

"You're on our planet now," said Sally, "and nothing makes sense here."

"On Earth, we have a little saying . . ." I began.

"WHEN IN ROME, DO AS THE ROMANS DO?" asked Mack.

"No. Earth — love it or leave it. Now, before I forget, there's one very important part of baseball that is necessary for you to . . . uh . . . assimilate. And that's baseball chatter."

"CHATTER?" Mack asked quizzically.

"Yes. While one team is trying to hit the ball and the other team is trying to catch the ball, everybody on both teams yells at one another."

"YOU MEAN THAT SILENCE IS NOT OB-SERVED DURING THE PLAYING OF THE GAME?"

"No way!" I said expertly. "It's much more fun when everybody hollers stuff at each other. You know, stuff like . . . uh, Corny help me out here."

"Stuff like, 'We want a pitcher, not a glass of water!' " Corny said.

The aliens gathered in a group for a minute talking this over.

"WE DO NOT UNDERSTAND," Mack said when they came out of their huddle. "WHAT DOES A GLASS OF WATER HAVE TO DO WITH BASEBALL?"

"You see," Corny explained. "A baseball pitcher throws the ball. When we eat, we'll have a pitcher of water, or some other drink. So it's like we're saying we want a whole pitcher, not just a glass of water. . . . Get it? It's a little joke."

Mack and his comrades looked at one another.

"VERY LITTLE JOKE," Mack said.

Sally stepped forward to offer another explanation. "We get really thirsty playing baseball."

"AH! NOW WE UNDERSTAND!" the aliens said. "SO YOU WANT A PITCHER, NOT JUST A GLASS OF WATER!"

"The point of chatter is that it doesn't much matter what you say," I explained. "You just want to get your team motivated and the other team rattled. I'm sure you guys assimilated a few things about baseball on your way over here. Let's hear you holler some stuff at me."

"WATCH ME BUNT THIS GOPHER BALL RIGHT UP YOUR ON-DECK CIRCLE!" one of the aliens shouted.

"I WILL SLIDE INTO THE PITCHER'S MOUND AND SCORE THE WINNING UMPIRE!" said another.

"HEY, FUNGO FACE! YOUR MOTHER IS SO

UGLY SHE SHOULD WEAR A CATCHER'S MASK!"
yelled a third.

"Now you're getting the hang of it!" I said. "Next, let me tell you about the infield fly rule. . . ."

"ENOUGH RULES. LET US BEGIN THE GAME."

"Hold on, Mack," I said. "We haven't even scratched the surface yet. We have to teach you about the hit-and-run, passed balls, double plays, tagging up, hitting to the opposite field, and negotiating a multi-year contract. Baseball is a very subtle and complex sport."

"I AM QUITE SURE IT IS," Mack said. "BUT WE CAN SCRATCH THAT SURFACE ANOTHER DAY. OUR TIME HERE IS GETTING SHORT. LET US PLAY A GAME NOW."

4
Play Ball!

Things were getting really weird. Picture this: There are three spaceships the size of houses floating beyond the outfield fence. At each of the nine field positions is a vending machine hovering over the ground. All sorts of strange beeps and lights are coming out of them. We're sitting in our dugout hoping to win the game so we can get a ride on a flying saucer. It was just too weird.

"What was that all about?" Corny shouted after the beeping stopped.

"OUR NATIONAL ANTHEM, OF COURSE," replied Mack.

Sally stepped up to the plate swinging her favorite piece of lumber, a Louisville Slugger with the name "Henry Aaron" carved into the barrel. She'd been using this bat for a few years now, and she said it felt just right in her hands. Most everybody else uses aluminum bats, but Sally doesn't like them. She loves the *craaaack* sound of a wooden bat striking a baseball.

When Sally first joined the SBDs, I didn't know how she would react to being called a second "baseman" so I called her the second "baseperson." Boy, was she mad! She said she didn't want to be treated differently from anybody else. So now she's our second baseman, and probably the best I've seen among kids our age.

Sally is such a serious hitter that she washes her bat after every game so she can see the marks that are made each time the bat hits the ball. That way, she knows how far up the barrel she's making contact, and if her swing is level. That's why we have Sally lead off for our team. She almost always gets wood on the ball.

"Let's go, Sally!" somebody called from the bench. "Get a hit!"

Sally tapped the bat against her right foot, and then her left. She was a little nervous, realizing that this was history in the making — she would be the first person in history to bat against someone from another planet.

"ARE YOU READY FOR A STRIKE IN, EARTH GIRL?"

"That's a strikeout, Mack," she said. "And no, I'm not. In fact, I'm going to knock this one clear to your planet."

"GIVEN THE COEFFICIENT OF RESTITUTION OF A BASEBALL, THAT IS HIGHLY UNLIKELY."

"Coefficient of huh?" Sally mumbled.

* * *

Lacking arms and legs, Mack couldn't very well go into a traditional pitcher's windup. Instead, the small lights on his upper torso began blinking, first slowly and then faster. At the same time, a series of beeps came out of him.

After a number of beeps, a baseball shot out of the hole in his middle, whistling through the air so fast it was impossible to see. A loud *whommmmmmp* echoed and the ball slammed perfectly into the corresponding hole in the belly of Wendy, who was playing catcher.

"STRIKE ONE!" shouted Wendy.

Sally's jaw dropped open and she shook her head with disbelief. In the dugout, we all gasped. Ray looked as if he was ready to hide under the bench.

"I didn't even see him throw it!" Sally complained.

"PERHAPS YOU WILL PAY MORE ATTENTION THIS TIME," Mack said as the ball zipped out of Wendy's belly and landed squarely back in his own.

Sally gritted her teeth and dug her toe more firmly into the batter's box.

The lights on Mack's torso began to blink again and he started beeping. I noticed a droplet of sweat trickling down Sally's bangs. She choked up on her bat and concentrated on the circular spot on Mack's belly where the ball would be coming from.

Whommmmmmp!

"STRIKE TWO!" Wendy shouted. Sally hadn't gotten the bat off her shoulder.

"Wait a minute! Wait a minute!" I yelled. This was ridiculous. I hopped off the bench and jogged out to the mound. "What was that?"

"A FASTBALL," said Mack matter-of-factly.

"You can say *that* again!"

"A FASTBALL," Mack repeated. "I CALCULATE IT TO HAVE TRAVELED AT A RATE OF SEVEN HUNDRED SEVENTY-THREE MILES PER

HOUR. THAT SOUND YOU HEARD WAS A SONIC BOOM, WHICH OCCURS IN YOUR EARTH AT-MOSPHERE WHEN AN OBJECT TRAVELS FASTER THAN THE SPEED OF SOUND — SEVEN HUNDRED SEVENTY MILES PER HOUR."

"You've got a built-in speed gun?" asked Corny. "Is that cool or what?"

"WOULD YOU LIKE TO SEE A CURVEBALL?" Mack asked.

"Wait a minute," Sally said, throwing her arms up in the air. "You can throw a ball seven hundred seventy-three miles an hour and you have a curveball, *too*?"

I walked back to the dugout, shaking my head. It occurred to me that we could actually lose this game.

Mack swiveled around so he was facing third base.

"BY SPINNING THE BALL SEVENTY-SEVEN REVOLUTIONS, I CALCULATE THAT I SHOULD BE ABLE TO THROW IT DIRECTLY TOWARD THIRD BASE AND HAVE IT CURVE ENOUGH TO

CROSS HOME PLATE WITHIN THE STRIKE ZONE."

"At least he isn't sneaky," Corny said to me on the bench.

Sally choked up farther on her bat. Instead of holding it at shoulder height, she brought it down to waist level. Smart move. If the ball is going to go directly in that hole in Wendy's belly, Sally might as well put the bat right there and she'll *have* to make contact.

Mack went into his beeping and flashing act. The ball rocketed out of his belly directly toward third base. About halfway there, it slowed down almost to a stop, changed direction, and swooped toward the plate like a dive-bombing plane.

Sally closed her eyes and gripped her bat as firmly as she could.

Craaaaaaack!

The ball struck with so much force that it sheared right through the barrel

of the bat, leaving Sally holding the splintered handle. The ball smacked into Wendy's belly and the head of the bat fell harmlessly on home plate.

"FOUL TIP! STRIKE THREE! NEXT BATTER!" Wendy shouted.

"Foul tip?!" cried Sally angrily. "Foul tip?! You ruined my Henry Aaron! This was my favorite bat."

"AS YOU EARTHLINGS SAY, THOSE ARE THE BREAKS," said Mack. "NEXT BATTER!"

With one out in the top of the first inning, Corny Kornbluth nervously walked to the plate. I could tell Corny was nervous because he wasn't cracking any jokes. He looked as if he was being led to prison.

Corny had one thing going for him — he used an aluminum bat. He knew a baseball couldn't break it, no matter how fast the pitcher could throw.

Choking up just like Sally did, Corny

squared around as if to bunt and held the bat directly in front of Wendy's belly. If one of us ever *did* put a ball into play, I couldn't imagine how these aliens could field it.

Mack beeped, flashed, and let fly. The ball zoomed out of his belly, and exploded toward the plate. *Whommmmmmp!* Shaken by the noise, Corny trembled and dipped the bat an inch below the spot he wanted to hold it. The ball ticked off the top of the bat, flying in a high arc behind the plate.

"FOUL BALL! STRIKE ONE!" yelled Wendy.

"Hey, you guys!" shouted Corny proudly. "I fouled one off!"

"Way to go, Corny," I shouted from the on-deck circle. "Straighten it out."

Corny rubbed some dirt on his hands and gripped the bat with renewed confidence.

Beep . . . Beep . . . Beep . . . Whommmmmmp!

This time Corny jerked the bat *up* an inch

and the ball ticked off the lower part of the barrel, slamming into the ground and out of play.

"FOUL BALL. STRIKE TWO," called Wendy.

Corny went into his crouch once again. This time he was determined to hold the bat steady. Mack beeped, flashed, boomed, and the ball exploded toward the plate.

Whommmmmmp Baaaaaaang!

"*Owwwwwwwwwwww!*" Corny screamed as the bat went flying out of his grip. "My hands!"

Corny fell to his knees, shaking his hands furiously. His face was twisted with pain. We all ran out to him, while the ball rolled slowly to the pitcher's mound. Mack sucked it up with his bellyhole and fired it to first base for the out.

"Corny," I said, cradling him in my arms. "Are you okay?"

"My whole body is buzzin', Bloop!" moaned

Corny. "I feel like a big tuning fork."

It wasn't looking good for the human race this night.

The rest of the team helped Corny to the bench while I walked up to the plate. I was thinking fast. Sally had the right idea when she held the bat out in front of Wendy's bellyhole, but the ball was moving so fast it broke her wooden bat in two. Corny tried using an aluminum bat, and the impact of ball against bat nearly took his hands off.

I knew that you can hit a fast pitch much harder than a slow pitch because the velocity of the ball is transferred from the ball to the bat during the collision. Mack pitched faster than anybody, so instead of squaring around to bunt as Sally and Corny had done, it would be better strategy to swing away.

I'd probably strike out, but at least I'd be giving it my best shot. And if I *could* actually make contact, I would really give the ball a ride.

"TWO OUTS," Mack announced. "ONE MORE OUT AND WE SWITCH SIDES."

"I know how to play the game, Mack," I said. I couldn't help but be a little annoyed now — these weird creatures land on our planet, play on our field, and do it better than we do.

I stepped up to the plate and gripped the bat all the way down on the handle. Then I began my usual routine. First I touched the bill of my cap and tapped the plate three times with my bat. Then I hitched up my jeans and rocked my knees forward twice. Finally, I took two practice cuts and stared hard at Mack.

"ARE YOU THIRSTY?" Mack asked. "WOULD YOU LIKE A GLASS OF WATER, OR PERHAPS AN ENTIRE PITCHER?"

"This is how I get ready," I said. "You've got your beeps and lights, and I've got my stuff that I have to do."

The old saying goes, "Keep your eye on the ball," but Mack threw the ball so hard it was impossible to see it. Still, I had been studying his delivery and thought I came up with a way to hit him.

With Sally and Corny, I noticed how long it took Mack's fastball to go from his to Wendy's bellyhole. A split second, to be sure, but even so it took a certain amount of time. I knew exactly where the ball would be crossing the plate. If I could listen to the beeps and time my swing perfectly, I could hit the ball to kingdom come even if I couldn't see it. I'd have to anticipate the pitch.

That was my theory, anyway.

Mack beeped, flashed, and I swung the bat as hard as I could.

Swish!

"STRIKE ONE!" Wendy called as the ball popped back into Mack's bellyhole.

"Hey, Bloop!" shouted Corny from the dugout. "I can feel the breeze from here!" Corny seemed to have recovered from his at-bat and was back to his usual self.

"Just a little late," I said to myself. "I started my swing on the fifth beep. This time I'll start on the fourth beep."

Mack began his flashing, beeping windup. On the fourth beep, I swung for the fences.

Swish!

"STRIKE TWO!" called Wendy.

"Bloop, you're embarrassing our whole planet up there," Corny shouted through cupped hands.

"Still too slow!" I said to myself as I stepped out of the batter's box for a moment. "Three beeps this time."

I touched my cap, tapped the plate, hitched up my pants, rocked my knees, took my practice cuts, and stared at Mack.

Beeeep . . . Beeeep . . . Beeeep . . .

Let me interrupt the story for just a moment here to tell you that I'm not the strongest kid in the world. I'm not even the strongest kid in Haddonfield, New Jersey. But this was the hardest swing I had ever taken. I brought the bat head around even before Mack released the ball. But by the time the bat got to the center of the plate, the ball was right there on top of it.

Craaaaaaack!!!!!!!

It didn't hurt my hands at all. It felt *good*. The ball took off like a bullet from a gun.

"Holy cow!" shouted Corny.

Everybody jumped off the bench. The aliens swiveled around to follow the ball in flight.

I just stood at the plate and stared. I had never hit a ball so hard or so far. It would have been a home run in Yankee Stadium.

The crack was still echoing across Crow's Woods when the ball landed way past the center field fence.

"That's outta here!" shouted Sally, clapping wildly. "You got *all* of that one, Bloopster!"

I trotted around the bases, feeling on top of the world.

"I think you're losing a little zip on your heater, Mack," I said as I rounded third base. "Maybe you'd better bring in a relief pitcher."

"NICE HIT," Mack said, unconcerned. "YOU ARE NOW LEADING, ONE RUN TO ZERO."

Ray was the first to greet me as I touched home plate. He grabbed my hand and pumped it, saying, "I knew you wouldn't let us lose, Bloop Jones! I knew you'd find a way!"

Winning was always important to Ray. Even when we were just playing a game for fun, he always took it very seriously. It seemed as if Ray could never relax and just have fun. Maybe it was because he was the worst player on our team. I have to admit that we only have him on the SBDs because he gets us free bats and balls and other cool stuff from his dad's sporting goods store.

"Lemme have a crack at him, Bloop," Ray begged. "Can I hit now?"

It wasn't Ray's turn to bat, but he had such a pleading look in his eyes that I told him to go ahead and give it his best shot. Maybe it would boost his confidence.

I told Ray to take his swing on the third beep, but once he got into the batter's box and saw the speed of Mack's pitches, he forgot my advice. He swung meekly at three fastballs from Mack, looking relieved when strike three hummed in and he could get out of the batter's box.

"THREE OUTS!" shouted Mack. "IN THE

MIDDLE OF THE FIRST INNING, THE SCORE IS HUMANS ONE, VISITORS COMING TO BAT. YOU SCORED ONE RUN ON ONE HIT, NO ERRORS, AND NOBODY LEFT ON BASE."

"You learn fast," I said as I grabbed my glove and ran out onto the field.

"THANK YOU!" Mack said.

5
CRAAAAAAAAAAACK!

As we took the field in the bottom of the first inning, we were amazed by two things. First, we were actually playing a game of baseball against a bunch of aliens from another planet who looked like large appliances! Second, we were *winning*!

I kicked at the dirt on the mound, feeling pretty good and thinking about how I was going to pitch to these creatures. Considering that they had no arms, they threw the ball pretty well. But how could they possibly hit? How could they even hold a bat?

That question was answered immediately when Mack hovered over to the plate as the leadoff hitter. He had inserted the nob end of a bat into his bellyhole so that it stuck straight out, like a flagpole off the side of a building.

I had to snicker. I've seen some pretty awful-looking batting stances in my time, but this one had to be the *worst*. I turned around and motioned for the outfield to move in a few steps. There was really no point in even *having* outfielders against these aliens, but I didn't want to humiliate anybody.

"Why don't you take a few practice swings?" I called out, trying to be helpful.

"NO, THANK YOU," Mack responded. "I AM QUITE PREPARED."

"I'll go easy on him," I said to myself as I went into my windup. I kicked up my leg, rocked back, and grooved one nice and soft right over the plate.

"Strike one!" Corny bellowed. It didn't even look as if Mack had the ability to swing the bat. Corny whipped the ball back to me, and I threw another one right down Broadway. Mack didn't move the bat.

"Strike two!"

At that point, Mack started beeping and flashing, just as he did when he was pitching. Only this time, his entire body started to rotate, pulling the bat around in a circle, slowly at first, then faster, until Mack was whirling around and around like an ice skater doing a spin.

"So they can swing a bat," I said as I went into my windup. "Well, let's see if he can hit this. . . ."

Craaaaaaccccccccccccccckkkkkkkkkkkkk!

I never saw the ball leave the bat. It was over the fence before I could even turn my

head around to watch it. Instead of in a lazy arc, it flew across the sky like a heat-seeking missile. As Mack started his home run glide, we all stared at the ball, still visible by the light of the moon.

"It's not coming down," Corny said, amazed. "I think he actually launched it into orbit."

Mack floated around the bases. He held the bat the whole time and dropped it when he reached home plate.

"HOME RUN. THAT MAKES ONE RUN FOR US AND ONE RUN FOR YOU."

"Nice shot," Sally commented. "You really creamed that one."

"THE BALL HAS NOT RETURNED TO EARTH YET, BUT BASED ON THE TRAJECTORY I HAVE CALCULATED IT WILL TRAVEL ONE HUNDRED FIFTEEN MILES. THAT MEANS IT WILL LAND IN HARRISBURG, PENNSYLVANIA."

Now I was getting mad. These aliens could not only *throw* the ball faster than the speed of sound, but they could *hit* it into the next state.

"Baseball is *our* game," I thought to myself. "These guys show up from nowhere and they're making us look like a bunch of jerks."

Next up was Wendy, who went into her beeping and spinning routine, until the bat was whipping around so fast you could barely see it. Corny put down two fingers. Maybe a curveball would fool — .

Thkkkkkkkkkkkkkk!

Wendy swung slightly under the ball and it ticked off the top of the bat, sending it straight into the air.

"I got it!" Corny yelled instinctively. He expertly pulled off his mask and tossed it out of the way so he wouldn't trip over it. Corny circled around, staring straight upward, waiting for the ball to come down.

It didn't. The ball just kept rising until it was so small it seemed to vanish. Wendy started up the line to first base.

"I don't have it! I don't have it!" Corny shouted desperately. "Where did it go?" Wendy was rounding second base.

"It disappeared," Ray said disgustedly. "She hit a lousy pop-up so high, it probably left Earth's atmosphere and burned up in outer space."

Wendy was approaching third base when Sally shouted, "Wait! I see it! It's coming back down!"

And so it was. A tiny dot at first, not much bigger than a star in the sky, it got larger and larger until it was clear that it was a baseball hurtling to Earth. Corny smacked his glove with his fist and circled about two feet in front of home plate.

"Corny! Don't try to catch it," yelled Sally. "If the ball is reentering the Earth's atmosphere it could be thousands of degrees hot. It will be like catching a burning coal!"

61

"I don't care!" Corny shouted, holding his mitt out and staring straight up in the sky. "I'm going for it!"

Corny considered himself something of an expert at catching pop-ups. He planted his feet and braced himself for the impact of ball against mitt. By now, Wendy was rounding third and heading home. The ball was coming down, and I could see that the lower half gave off a fiery red glow. Corny held out his mitt, squinting his eyes slightly.

Fffffffffffffffffffffffffffffftttttt!

The ball ripped through the mitt like a cookie cutter going through dough. It smashed into the dirt and kept going, burrowing about a foot and a half deep into the infield. Wendy crossed the plate.

Corny held up his mitt. It had a perfect baseball-sized hole in it. Smoke was pouring from the edges. There was also smoke coming out of the hole in the ground where the ball landed.

"HOME RUN!" shouted Wendy. "THAT'S TWO RUNS FOR US AND ONE FOR YOUR TEAM."

Corny kept looking at his mitt and shaking his head.

"Something tells me this isn't going to be our night," he said. I could see he was upset that his favorite catcher's mitt was ruined.

Sally grabbed a shovel from behind the backstop and dug the ball out of the ground. One half was white and the other half was blackened and smoldering.

The next alien batter — Burger King, or B.K. as we had nicknamed him — hovered over to the plate, beeping and flashing and whipping the bat around so fast that I could feel the breeze on the pitcher's mound. Corny grabbed an old glove off the bench and trotted out to the pitcher's mound.

"I think we've met our match, Bloopster," he said. "These guys play like they're not human or something."

"That's because they're *not* human," I replied. "I think we may have to resort to our secret weapon."

"You don't mean . . ."

"Yes," I said in a hushed tone. "The Blooper."

I haven't told you how I got the nickname "Bloop." I hate to tell people this, but my real name is Marvin. Everybody calls me Bloop because of my special pitch, the Blooper ball. Instead of trying to throw hard, I just kind of lob the ball to the plate.

To batters, the Blooper ball looks like a watermelon hovering in the air for an eternity. But it's a very tough pitch to hit, and you look silly lunging at it. It's also very difficult to get over the plate. A guy named Rip Sewell used to throw it for the Pittsburgh Pirates in the 1940s. He called it his "Eephus pitch."

Corny trotted back to the plate, put his mask on, and settled into his crouch. B.K. was still whirling the bat around. I jammed the ball deep into my palm and went into my regular windup, rocking back as though I was going to throw a fastball or curve. But instead of releasing the ball as my arm was snapping down, I released it as my arm was still on its way up.

The ball lofted slowly in the air and floated in a high, tantalizing arc toward the plate. It hung in the air for what seemed like an hour. B.K. was whipping the bat around until the ball finally crossed into the strike zone and . . .

Whaaaaaaaaaam!

I didn't even turn around. If I had, I

would have seen my secret weapon on its way to Harrisburg.

It didn't look as if I was going to fool them with Bloopers, curves, fastballs, or anything else. At least the aliens were getting *under* the ball, I thought to myself. If one of these guys ever hit a line drive at somebody, it could take their head off.

"THIS BASEBALL IS QUITE FUN!" said B.K. as he rounded the bases. "NO WONDER YOU HAVE DUBBED IT YOUR NATIONAL PASTIME!"

The next alien batter glided up to the plate, blinking and flashing like the others. Corny dropped down one finger and I whipped in a fastball.

Thwaaaaaaack!

It was gone, of course. I couldn't even say, "Going . . . going . . . gone," because it was gone before I got the first "going" out of my mouth.

"That's it. All our baseballs are in Pennsylvania now," Corny said sadly. "I guess the game's over."

"NONSENSE," Mack said. "WE TOOK THE PRECAUTION OF BRINGING ALONG SOME OF OUR OWN." With that, a light on his chest blinked and a pile of baseballs rolled out his bellyhole, like gumballs from a vending machine.

Just then I noticed Ray sitting on second base with his hand covering his face. I walked over to him. It was obvious that he was crying.

"What's the matter, Ray?" I asked. "You okay?"

"We lost, Bloop!" he sobbed. "We've been playing on this field for a couple of years now and we've never lost. We're not supposed to lose! *You're* not supposed to lose."

So that was it. I signaled time out and

sat on the ground next to Ray. He wiped his sleeve across his eyes.

"Ray, do you know who had the highest lifetime batting average in baseball history?"

"I don't know. Babe Ruth?" he blubbered.

"No. Ty Cobb. Three seventy-six."

I pride myself on my knowledge of baseball statistics. You'd be surprised how often it comes in handy to prove a point in a discussion, even if it has nothing to do with baseball.

"So what?" asked Ray.

"So that means that for every one thousand times Cobb went to the plate, he got three hundred seventy-six hits."

"So?"

"Well," I continued, "it also means that for every one thousand times he went to the plate, Cobb *failed* to get a hit six hundred twenty-four times. Most of the time the man batted, he *didn't* get a hit.

He struck out, or he popped up, or something. He failed more than six out of every ten times he tried. And this is the best hitter in baseball history. Everybody *else* did even worse than that."

"Huh!" Ray had stopped sniffling and was listening intently.

"And you know what else, Ray? Ty Cobb's teams were lousy. In all those years he was a superstar with Detroit, do you know how the Tigers did?"

"No."

"They came in seventh place twice and sixth place five times. They came in fourth place four times, third place five times and second place three times. With the great Ty Cobb, the best hitter in baseball history, Detroit only won three lousy pennants. And you know what else? Each of those three times they lost the World Series. Ty Cobb never won a World Series."

"Huh. I didn't know that," Ray said.

"Do you understand the point I'm trying to make, Ray?"

"That Ty Cobb wasn't as good as everybody says he was?"

"No, he was just as good as everybody says he was. But as good as he was, he still had to put up with a lot of failure and loss. *Nobody* gets a hit every time they step up to the plate. Nobody wins every game. Not even the best player in history. That's life. You just have to go out there and do your best and if you don't come out on top, come back and try again tomorrow."

I was about to tell Ray about all the 316 games Cy Young lost during his Hall of Fame career, but I think he got the message. I gave Ray a pat on the back.

"Besides," I whispered, "this game isn't over yet. I have a plan."

6
A Deal's a Deal

One by one the aliens hovered up to the plate and smashed my best pitches out of sight. Fastballs, curveballs, even Blooper balls made no difference. These guys were simply unstoppable. Ten runs. Twenty runs. Thirty runs. And it was only the first inning!

It looked as if it was going to be a long night. At least I had been right about one thing — I really *didn't* need outfielders. There was nothing for them to catch! These aliens couldn't hit anything less than a home run if they tried.

That's where my secret plan came in. If all these aliens could do is hit home runs, they'd never make any outs. And if they never made any outs, the game would never get past the first inning. And if the game never gets past the first inning, we can never lose!

I thought to myself: *"I'm a genius!"* If there's one thing I hate to do, it's lose. Even more than Ray.

Slaaaaaaam! Craaaaaack! Thwaaaaack! The balls were flying out of Crow's Woods as if there was a war going on. I didn't care. It was a pleasure watching superior hitters practicing their art. I looked at my watch and saw that it was 10:27. It was only a matter of time.

When the score reached 35–1, Mack hovered out to the mound.

"WE MUST LEAVE YOUR PLANET NOW," he said. "WE WANT TO THANK YOU FOR TEACHING US THE WONDERFUL GAME OF BASEBALL."

"You're completely welcome," I said. "So which one of your spaceships do we get a ride in?"

"HA-HA. THAT MUST BE MORE OF YOUR EARTH HUMOR," Mack said. "OUR AGREEMENT WAS THAT YOU COULD GET A RIDE IN A SPACESHIP IF YOU WON THE GAME. THE SCORE IS THIRTY-FIVE TO ONE IN OUR FAVOR."

"Gentlemen," I said as everyone gathered around. "Baseball is a funny game. There's no clock ticking away the final seconds, like football or basketball or soccer. There are no time limits. The game goes on until the final out. As the famous Earth philosopher Yogi Berra once said, 'It ain't over till it's over.' And unless I counted wrong, we're still in the first inning here.

So it ain't over. If you guys have to leave, that's okay with us. But that means you forfeit the game and we get a ride in one of your ships."

"FORFEIT?" Mack asked.

"Maybe you didn't assimilate that on your trip over here," I said, pulling my trusty copy of *Official Baseball Rules* out of my back pocket. "It says right here in rule number four point fifteen . . . 'A game may be forfeited to the opposing team when a team refuses to continue play during a game unless the game has been suspended or terminated by the umpire.' "

"So we win!" Corny shouted, jumping in the air. "All right! What a game!"

"B-B-BUT HUMANS IN OUR SPACESHIPS WOULD BE OUT OF THE QUESTION. IT'S IMPOS-SIBLE. WE COULD NEVER ALLOW IT."

"Mack, a deal is a deal. Or don't you stick to your word on your planet?"

* * *

The nine aliens silently hovered a few feet away and discussed the situation in hushed beeps and lights. Sally pulled me aside and whispered into my ear.

"Bloop, are you crazy?" she said. "I want a spaceship ride as much as you do. But let's think this thing through, okay? They're getting a little upset, don't you think? If these aliens can throw a ball eight hundred miles an hour and hit home runs that land in Harrisburg, what do you think they might do if they get angry? Personally, I don't know. But I'll tell you this much — I don't want to find out."

I thought about what Sally said. She had made a good point. It wouldn't be worth getting killed just to get a ride in a spaceship. I walked quickly over to the aliens to talk things over before they did anything drastic.

"Hey, guys!" I said quietly. "Look, we're peace-loving people. It was a pleasure just engaging with you on the field of athletic competition. Forget about the ride."

Maybe I was too late. As a group, the aliens turned toward me. I was expecting the worst. Like 800-mile-an-hour split-finger fastballs shooting out of their belly-holes.

"A DEAL IS A DEAL," Mack said. "THAT IS AS TRUE ON OUR PLANET AS IT IS ON YOURS. YOU DEFEATED US FAIRLY AND SQUARELY. LET US MOVE TO THE SHIP IN CENTER FIELD FOR A RIDE. THEN WE MUST LEAVE."

"All riiiiiiiiiiiight!" everybody shouted.

7
The Ride of Our Lives

One by one we walked up the ramp of the spaceship. As I entered the door, Sally suddenly stopped and grabbed my arm. She had the look of terror in her eyes.

"Bloop! Now I see it," Sally whispered. "They didn't want to learn how to play baseball!"

"They didn't?"

"No! It was all a trick! They just wanted to get us into their spaceship! Don't you see? We're not getting a ride — we're being kidnapped! They're going to take us back to their planet and do who-knows-what with us! I saw this on an episode of *The Twilight Zone* once. They don't care about baseball in the least!"

Sally is probably the smartest person I know. She always gets A's in all her classes and she never even seems to study. It never occurred to me that the aliens had anything up their sleeves.

I turned to bolt out of the spaceship, but my path was blocked by Mack. The hatch was closing behind him.

"MR. BLOOP," he said in his ominous voice. "THERE WAS ONE THING I FORGOT TO TELL YOU BEFORE YOU ENTERED THE SHIP."

I gulped. Sally was right. I had fallen for the aliens' trick. How could I have been so stupid?

"What was that, Mack?" I asked.

"TY COBB'S LIFETIME BATTING AVERAGE WAS NOT THREE SEVENTY-SIX. IT WAS THREE SIXTY-SEVEN. AND IF HE HAD NOT BEEN

SURROUNDED BY SUCH LOUSY TEAMMATES, THE DETROIT TIGERS WOULD HAVE CERTAINLY WON MORE PENNANTS."

Sally and I breathed a big sigh of relief. These guys *did* love baseball!

Have you ever been on Space Mountain at Disneyland? Well, this spaceship made Space Mountain look like a tricycle ride. The ship took off straight up like an elevator, but suddenly it swooped and dove like a bird, so the nine of us were completely weightless.

Our bodies flew around the cabin, bumping into the walls and each other. There were no lights inside, so we had no idea who we were slamming into. All I could hear was hysterical giggling, and I suspect that some of it was coming from the aliens.

The ride lasted about ten minutes, and then the ship gently floated down as we all settled to the floor in a big heap.

Corny summed up the ride by saying, "This is the most fun I've ever had while on the verge of puking!"

As we touched down in center field, we gathered around Mack and the other aliens to say good-bye. It was Mack who spoke first.

"WE HOPE YOU ENJOYED THE RIDE. WE WOULD LIKE TO GIVE YOU SOMETHING AS A TOKEN OF OUR APPRECIATION FOR TEACHING US YOUR WONDERFUL GAME."

Mack's lights blinked and a few seconds later a baseball rolled out of his bellyhole.

I picked it up and looked at it. Between the red seams were some markings. Looking closely, I could see that the ball said: "McDonald," "Burger King," "Wendy," "Taco Bell," and other fast-food names.

"You signed it!" I exclaimed. "You know, I've got some baseballs at home with the

autographs of major leaguers. But I'm going to treasure this one more than all the others."

Sally picked up a clean ball from the ground and pulled a pen out of her pocket. She wrote her name on the ball and passed it around to each of us. When everybody had signed, I put the ball in Mack's belly-hole. "Here," I said. "We want you to have this, too."

"THANK YOU, EARTH CHILDREN," Mack said seriously. "PERHAPS WE'LL MEET AGAIN . . . AT THE WORLD SERIES!"

"Correction," I replied. "The Intergalactic Series."

"So you think you'll come back to visit us sometime?" asked Ray.

"CERTAINLY. WE OBVIOUSLY NEED TO LEARN MORE ABOUT THE FINE POINTS OF BASEBALL. AND THERE IS ONE MORE ASPECT OF YOUR CIVILIZATION THAT WE WISH TO

BRING BACK TO OUR HOMELAND, IF YOU WILL TEACH IT TO US."

"Anything," I said. "What is it?"

"FOOTBALL."

We all gulped.

8
The Whole Truth

I took off my sneakers and tiptoed into the house, being careful not to step on the floorboards that creaked. The clock on the living room wall read 11:34.

"Marvin!" shouted my mom, stopping me in my tracks. She always calls me Marvin when she's angry. "Where *were* you? I was worried sick!"

"What do you mean, Mom?" I asked innocently. "I've been up in my room playing video games all night. I just came downstairs for a drink of water."

"Tell your mother the truth, Bloop."

Uh-oh. Dad's here, too.

"Okay, I know when I'm nabbed," I said, throwing my hands in the air. "Do you want me to make a long story short or a short story long?"

"Just tell us what happened, son. And none of your tall tales, now."

"Well, the honest truth is that me and the gang were out playing some ball when these aliens from another planet landed near Crow's Woods. They wanted to know how to play baseball, and we taught 'em. You should have seen 'em pitch and hit, Dad. It was amazing! They could throw the ball eight hundred miles an hour and hit it into Pennsylvania. Anyway, after the game they gave us a ride in one of their cool spaceships and we all autographed a ball for them to take home to their planet."

"Bloop?"

"Yes, Mom?"

"Go upstairs now."

"G'night, Mom and Dad," I said, winking at them as I went up to my room.

9
The Next Day . . .

The following report interrupted the television news in Harrisburg, Pennsylvania. . . .

"The Harrisburg police reported a most unusual occurrence last night. As many as fifteen baseballs landed on the city, and they appear to have come from miles away. No injuries have been reported, but several of the baseballs crashed through roofs, causing some property damage. The police don't know where these baseballs came from

and the best guess right now is that they were dropped from airplanes. At this point, nobody knows why.

We will break into our regular programming as more details become available. . . ."

About the Author

Dan Gutman knows a lot about baseball. He has written six books about the history of the game. Two of his most popular books are *Baseball's Greatest Games* and *Baseball's Biggest Bloopers*.

They Came from Center Field is his first fictional story, and the first one written for younger readers.

In addition to writing books, Mr. Gutman appears on radio and TV talk shows sharing his baseball stories. He likes to visit classrooms and talk to students about his favorite sport and how it helped him become a writer. He has always loved baseball, but when he was growing up he wasn't a good player. "I was afraid of getting hit with the ball," he says. But he didn't let that stop him from enjoying the game and learning everything he could about it.

Mr. Gutman lives in Haddonfield, New Jersey, with his wife, Nina, and son, Sam.